To Joshua,
Happy Easter
Love Grammie
a Grampa Joe
2004

Zachary's Ball

Matt Tavares

CANDLEWICK PRESS
CAMBRIDGE, MASSACHUSETTS

The publisher gratefully acknowledges that references to
Fenway Park, along with the Boston Red Sox name, uniform, likeness, and logos,
are used by permission of the Boston Red Sox.

First paperback edition 2002

The Library of Congress has cataloged the hardcover edition as follows:

Tavares, Matt.
Zachary's ball / Matt Tavares. — 1st ed.
p.   cm.
Summary: Dad takes Zachary to his first Boston Red Sox game where
they catch a ball and something magical happens.
ISBN 0-7636-0730-4 (hardcover)
[1. Baseball—Fiction. 2. Boston Red Sox (Baseball team)—Fiction.]
I. Title.
PZ7.T211427Zac   2000
[E]— dc21   99-34798

ISBN 0-7636-1768-7 (paperback)

2 4 6 8 10 9 7 5 3

Printed in Hong Kong

This book was typeset in Memphis.
The illustrations were done in pencil.

Candlewick Press
2067 Massachusetts Avenue
Cambridge, Massachusetts 02140

visit us at www.candlewick.com

To Barbara Gagel

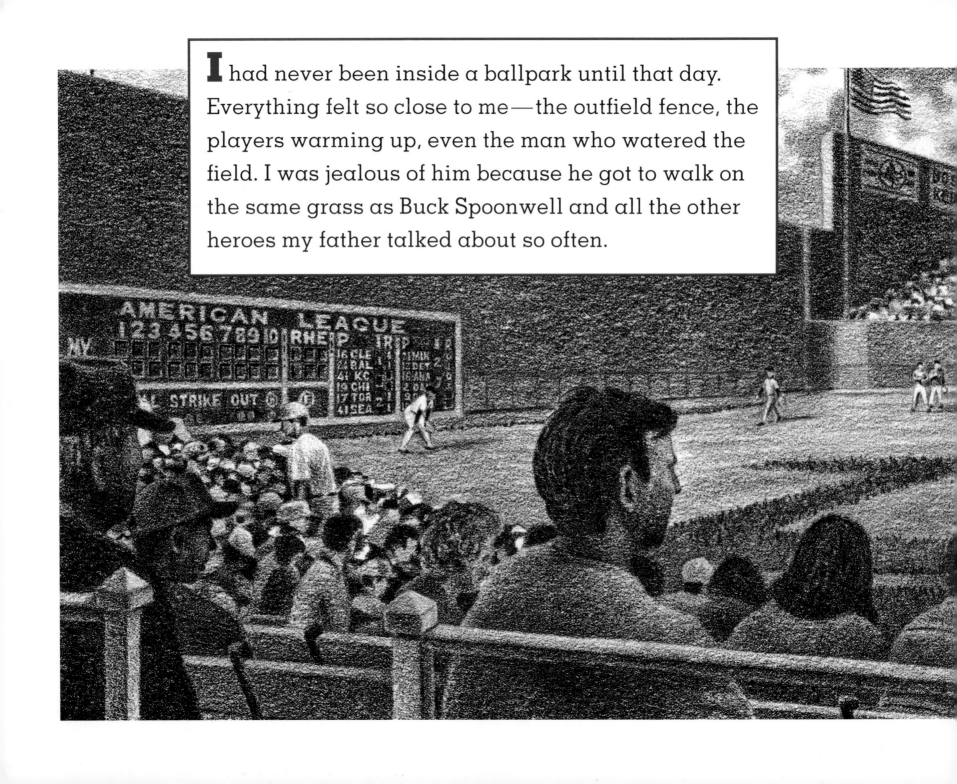

I had never been inside a ballpark until that day. Everything felt so close to me—the outfield fence, the players warming up, even the man who watered the field. I was jealous of him because he got to walk on the same grass as Buck Spoonwell and all the other heroes my father talked about so often.

I remember everybody clapping and hollering when Boston came up to bat.

Hundreds of people in the bleachers chanted in unison, "Let's go Sox! Let's go Sox!"

Buck Spoonwell was up first. "Hit a home run, Buck!" my father shouted.

"Let's go Buck!" I yelled as loud as I could.

On the first pitch, Buck took a mighty swing. But he did not hit a home run. Instead, he popped the ball straight up into the sky. The crowd groaned.

But then, suddenly, the wind picked up and carried the ball right toward us.

My father stood up. So did all the other grownups.
I stood up too, even though I was too little to catch
the ball. Once all the jumping and yelling stopped,
my father sat down, and with a big smile, he held in
front of me a beautiful white baseball.

As he handed me the ball, something unbelievable
happened.

All of a sudden, I was no longer sitting with my father. I was standing on the pitcher's mound, dressed in a Red Sox uniform.

"One more strike and we win, kid," said Skip Johnson, the manager, as he handed me the ball and returned to the dugout.

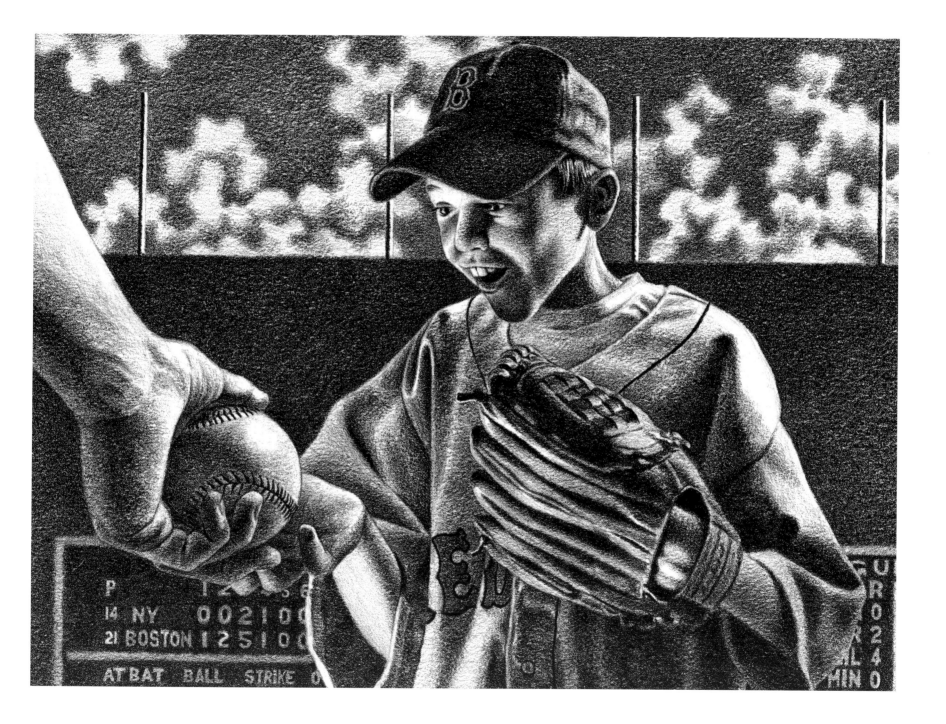

I looked at the catcher, crouched down behind the plate, waiting for my pitch. He gave me some sort of sign, but I didn't know what it meant, so I just reared back and threw the ball as hard as I could. The hitter swung as hard as he could, but the ball whizzed past him. Strike three. The Sox win!

The catcher ran out to the mound to give me the game ball. As he handed it to me, suddenly I was back in the stands with my father. It seemed as though no time had passed.

"Dad!" I exclaimed. "This baseball is magic!"

My father smiled. "They're all magic," he said.

I wrote my name on the baseball as soon as I got home that day. That night, I took my ball to bed with me, and each night, from then on, I dreamed about baseball.

One night, I was standing in left field at Fenway Park when New York's best hitter blasted a deep fly ball right toward me. I ran as fast as I could and dove for it, feeling the smack of the ball in my glove as I skidded across the outfield grass.

Another night, I struck out the final batter in the seventh game of the World Series. My teammates all ran out to the mound and held me above their shoulders while thousands of Red Sox fans stormed the field.

Then, one day, my baseball was gone. I looked in the drawer in my desk where I usually kept it. I looked all over my room. For weeks, I looked everywhere. But it was nowhere to be found.

A few months passed, and finally, I gave up.

I still dreamed of baseball, though. And every summer, I spent my Saturday afternoons at the ballpark, rooting for Boston . . .

. . . always hoping that another ball might come my way.

Years later, I was taking a walk in Boston down by the ballpark. The heat was unbearable, so I stopped to rest in a tiny spot of shade. I gazed up at the big wall in front of me. I heard the sound of cheering fans from inside the park.

Just then, out of the sky came a glowing white baseball — a towering home run, hit over the wall. I reached up and it fell gracefully into my outstretched hands. As I spun the dusty ball around, I thought I saw two faded words, written in a child's handwriting —

Zachary's Ball

Quickly, I tried to brush the dust away so I could read it more clearly. But as the dust vanished into the air, so did the words.

Holding my new baseball, I thought back to the day when my father took me to my first game. I remembered the gift he had given me. Now, I had caught a ball myself—I couldn't wait to tell him.

As I turned to head home, I noticed a young girl holding her father's hand. She was staring at my baseball.

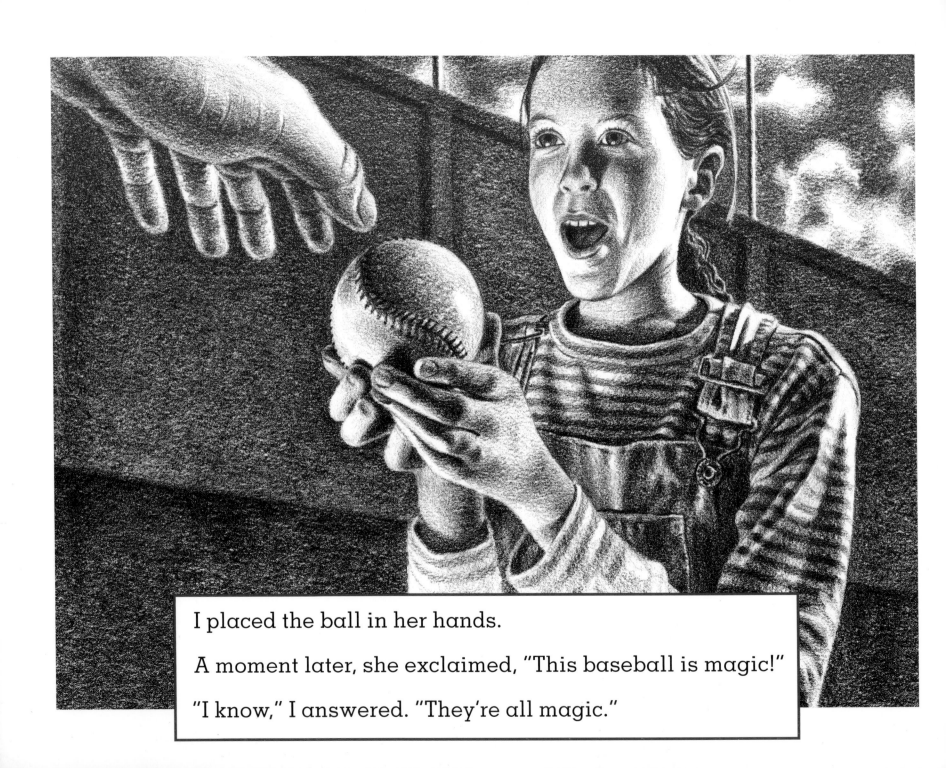

I placed the ball in her hands.

A moment later, she exclaimed, "This baseball is magic!"

"I know," I answered. "They're all magic."